# Magic
## Animal Friends

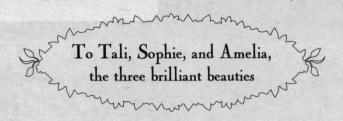

To Tali, Sophie, and Amelia,
the three brilliant beauties

## Special thanks to Valerie Wilding

No part of this publication may be reproduced, stored in a retrieval
system, or transmitted in any form or by any means, electronic,
mechanical, photocopying, recording, or otherwise, without written
permission of the publisher. For information regarding permission,
write to Working Partners Limited, Stanley House, St. Chad's Place,
London WC1X 9HH, United Kingdom.

ISBN 978-0-545-68648-8

Text copyright © 2014 by Working Partners Limited
Illustrations © 2014 by Working Partners Limited

Series author: Daisy Meadows

All rights reserved. Published by Scholastic Inc., 557 Broadway,
New York, NY 10012, by arrangement with Working Partners
Limited. Series created by Working Partners Limited, London.

12 11 10 9 8 7 6 5 4 3 2 1      15 16 17 18 19 20/0

Printed in the U.S.A.                              40
First printing, June 2015

# Bella Tabbypaw in Trouble

Daisy Meadows

Scholastic Inc.

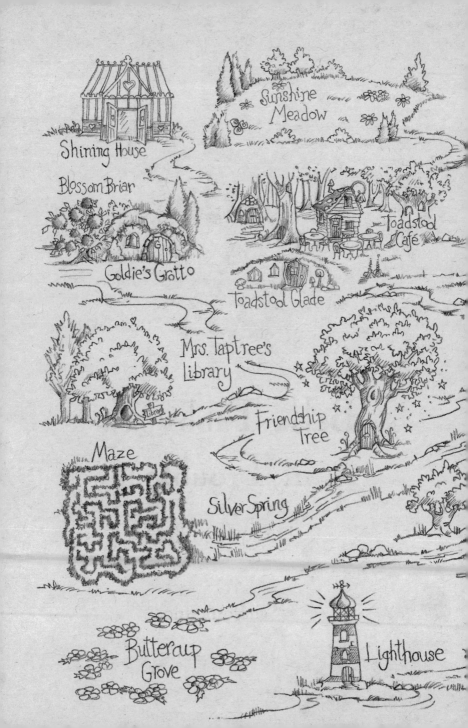

Shining House

Sunshine Meadow

Blossom Briar

Goldie's Grotto

Toadstool Café

Toadstool Glade

Mrs. Taptree's Library

Friendship Tree

Maze

Silver Spring

Butterup Grove

Lighthouse

# Map of Friendship Forest

Ace Air Travel

Windmill

Mr. Cleverfeather's Inventing Shed

Muddlepups' Den

Treasure Tree

Sparkly Falls

Featherbills' Barge

Waterwheel

Entrance to the Caverns

Swamp

Grizelda's Tower

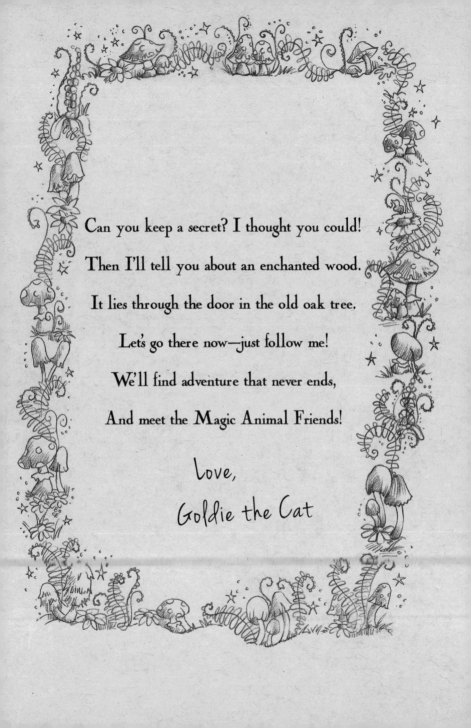

Can you keep a secret? I thought you could!

Then I'll tell you about an enchanted wood.

It lies through the door in the old oak tree.

Let's go there now—just follow me!

We'll find adventure that never ends,

And meet the Magic Animal Friends!

Love,
Goldie the Cat

# Contents

# CHAPTER ONE

# Kittens!

Lily Hart couldn't tear herself away from the box of kittens her dad had just brought into the examining room. Neither could her best friend, Jess Forester!

Lily's parents ran the Helping Paw Wildlife Hospital in Brightley, the town where the two girls lived. Jess and her dad

lived in the house across from the hospital. They'd found the kittens that morning in their shed and brought them straight to Helping Paw.

"I'll just check them over," said Mr. Hart.

He picked up each of the four kittens in turn, checking their eyes and teeth. When he put the smallest one back in the box, she rolled over on her back and meowed, showing the tip of a tiny pink tongue. Lily tickled her tummy.

"We were amazed to find them," Mr. Forester said. "Jess heard barking and saw

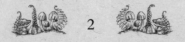

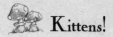 

a dog chasing a cat away from the shed. It must have been the kittens' mother. When she didn't come back, we looked inside and found the kittens."

"We've put flyers inside everyone's mailboxes to find out who the cat belongs to," Jess added. "But we knew that this was the best place to bring the kittens!"

"I'm glad you did," said Lily, picking up one of the soft, wriggling creatures. It batted a paw at her dark hair, making them all laugh.

"The kittens will be fine with warmth and milk," Mr. Hart said. He showed the

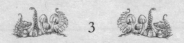

girls how to feed them with
drops squeezed from tiny
pipettes, then he and Mr.
Forester went into the
house to join Mrs. Hart
for a cup of tea.

The kittens climbed
over one another,
trying to reach
the milk.

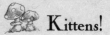 

"They're hungry!" laughed Jess.

When they were full, the kittens
cuddled together and fell asleep.

"I wonder who your mother is," said
Lily, stroking a kitten with a white tip on
its tail. "We already know one mysterious
cat, don't we, Jess?"

The two friends shared a smile, thinking
of their magical cat friend, Goldie. She

came from Friendship Forest, a secret
world of talking animals, and had taken
the girls on adventures there. An evil
witch called Grizelda wanted to drive
the animals out of the forest so she could
have it for herself, and Lily and Jess had
helped stop her on several occasions.

"I wonder when we'll see Goldie
again," said Jess.

As soon as she had spoken, the girls heard
a soft *tap-tap-tap* at the window. They looked
up to see a beautiful cat pawing at the glass.
She had golden fur and eyes as green as
grass in morning sunshine.

"Goldie!" cried
Lily, opening
the window.
"We were
just thinking
about you!"

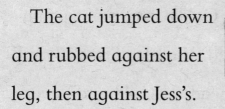

The cat jumped down
and rubbed against her
leg, then against Jess's.

"You know what this means, don't
you?" said Lily.

Jess nodded excitedly. "Whenever
Goldie visits, it's time for another
adventure in Friendship Forest!"

Goldie meowed at them. The girls knew she wanted them to follow her!

"We're coming, Goldie," cried Lily. She quickly checked that the kittens were all right and then the girls ran outside.

They followed Goldie over the stepping-stones that crossed Brightley Stream, and into Brightley Meadow. Goldie ran over to the Friendship Tree and it immediately burst into life. New leaves sprang from the dried twigs and blossoms burst into bloom. Birds sang sweetly among the branches. The girls had seen this happen

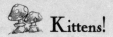 

before, but they still grinned at each other, wide-eyed with delight.

Goldie patted some letters carved into the tree trunk. Jess and Lily knew what the letters said, and that if they spoke the words aloud, magic would begin!

They held hands and said together, "Friendship Forest!"

A door as high as the girls' shoulders appeared in the trunk. Lily reached for the leaf-shaped handle and opened it.

Shimmering golden light shone from inside. Ducking down, Jess and Lily followed Goldie through the door. They

felt a familiar tingling
sensation all over. *We're
shrinking*, Jess thought
excitedly.

The light faded. They
were in a sun-dappled
clearing surrounded
by tall trees. Around the
edge were the little cottages where
the animals of Friendship Forest lived.

"We're back!" said Lily, her brown eyes
shining.

"And we're so glad you are," said a soft
voice.

The girls turned to see Goldie standing

upright, wearing a glistening scarf.

Because the girls had shrunk, she now

stood as tall as their shoulders.

Beside Goldie was a family of three

tabby cats—two adults and a little kitten.

Their silvery fur was swirled with dark gray. The girls recognized the kitten—they had met her on their very first visit to Friendship Forest. She carried a backpack on her back, and a pair of odd-looking binoculars dangled around her neck. She stared at the girls in amazement.

Goldie hugged Jess and Lily, then introduced them to the cats.

"This is Mr. and Mrs. Tabbypaw," she said. "As you girls know, I was once a stray in the human world. When I first found my way to Friendship Forest, the Tabbypaws looked after me. You're

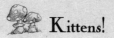 

all very special to me, so I wanted you
to meet each other."

"We're so pleased to meet you, Jess and
Lily," said Mrs. Tabbypaw. "You're such
wonderful friends to all the animals."

"Yes, indeedy," said Mr. Tabbypaw.
"We heard you stopped that witch
from ruining our lovely forest. Three
times, in fact!"

"Dad! Dad!" said the kitten.

"Oh, this is Bella," said Mr. Tabbypaw.
"She's excited to meet you, too!"

"I saw you when you first came to
Friendship Forest!" said the kitten. "We

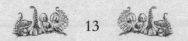

live far away in Buttercup Grove, and guess what? Tonight I'm having my first ever sleepover in Goldie's grotto!"

Mr. and Mrs. Tabbypaw had to leave so they'd be home before dark. They hugged and kissed Bella.

"Good-bye, Jess and Lily," they said. "It was wonderful to meet you. Bye, Goldie!"

They disappeared into the trees.

"Let's go to the Toadstool Café," Goldie said.

"Ooh, yes!" said Bella. "Jess and Lily, can you come, too? And to the sleepover?

Can you? You could tell me stories about

your world. I love hearing about new

things. Please?"

"You would be very welcome," smiled

Goldie.

Jess looked at Lily. "What about it?"

she said. "Time stands still while we're in

Friendship Forest, remember? We can stay

as long as we like."

"We'd love to!" said Lily.

Bella danced around in a circle and

cheered. "Hooray!"

## CHAPTER TWO

# Strange Sounds

Bella chattered as they made their way to the Toadstool Café.

"I love exploring," she said, peering at the wild flowers growing around the clearing. "Ooh! A bumblebee! Have you ever seen so many stripes?"

"Take a closer look with your binoculars," Lily suggested.

Bella giggled. "These aren't binoculars," she said. "They're night goggles, for seeing in the dark. Mr. Cleverfeather, the owl, invented them."

"When Bella grows up she'll have perfect night vision, like me," Goldie explained, "but she can't see properly in the dark yet."

Lily was about to reply when she heard a grunt. "What was that?" she asked. "It came from behind that starflower bush."

Jess went to look, but didn't see anyone. "That's strange," she said.

Soon they arrived at the Toadstool Café. The tables and umbrellas that dotted around outside were too small for the girls, so they sat on the mossy ground instead. As Bella ran around exploring the glade, Goldie came over to talk to the girls.

"Jess, Lily," she said quietly. "Remember that grunt we heard, from behind the starflower bush?"

They nodded.

"Earlier today," Goldie continued, "the

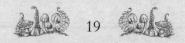

Tabbypaws and I heard strange sounds in the forest, rather like that grunt."

Jess frowned. "Could it have been the Boggits?"

The Boggits were the mean, filthy helpers of Grizelda the witch. She'd promised the Boggits a dirty, muddy new home if they helped her get rid of all the animals in Friendship Forest.

Before Goldie could reply, there was a loud crash from inside the café. She ran inside, while Jess and Lily kneeled to peer through the doorway.

Mr. and Mrs. Longwhiskers, the owners

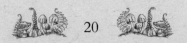

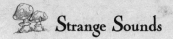 

of the café, were scratching their ears and staring at a heap of saucepans on the floor.

"What happened?" Mrs. Longwhiskers wondered aloud. "They were on the draining board by the window a second ago."

The cat's ears twitched thoughtfully as she came back outside to join the girls. "Something strange is going on in Friendship Forest," Goldie said. "I wonder what."

An hour later, Goldie, Bella, and the girls arrived at Goldie's grotto. It was a cave in another beautiful clearing. Beside the cave grew the Blossom Briar, a tall bush with colorful flowers as big as footballs. The girls knew that the Blossom Briar was connected to every flower in Friendship Forest. As long as it was healthy, the flowers would bloom, too.

Goldie opened the red front door that had a window the shape of a letter G, and they all went inside. On the mossy floor was a comfy bed, a squishy armchair, a table, and a fat, round footstool.

They ate pumpkin and pine nut soup with wild garlic bread, then curled up on the floor in a nest of quilts, blankets, and piles of soft cushions. Bella put her night goggles into her backpack and hung it on a hook, then clambered onto Jess's lap.

"It's so cozy and comfortable," said
Jess, stroking the kitten.

Bella started to purr. "Tell me stories
about the human world!" she said.

Lily told Bella all about the wildlife
hospital. When she finished, Bella said,
"More!" so Jess told tales about school
and the funny things their teacher said.

"More! More!" said Bella.

"I know," said Goldie, "I'll tell you the legend of Friendship Forest."

"What's a legend?" asked Bella.

"A very old story," said Goldie, "but we don't know if it's really true."

"Ooh!" said Bella.

So Goldie began. "Deep beneath Friendship Forest are many long-lost tunnels . . ."

"Wow!" said Bella, eyes wide. "Who lives there?"

"Nobody knows," said Goldie. "The legend tells that the tunnels are filled with wonderful jewels, some as small as apple seeds, and some as big as a kitten!"

"I'd love to explore the tunnels and find some jewels," said Bella dreamily. She yawned and wriggled into a tighter ball. In a moment, she was asleep.

Goldie giggled. "I'll finish that legend another time."

Jess carefully lifted Bella out of her lap and onto a quilt. Her paws twitched. "I think she's dreaming," Jess whispered with a grin.

The girls and Goldie snuggled down, too. They were just drifting off when they heard a rough, gruff sound outside.

"Hegga hegga!" it went.

Jess and Lily sat bolt upright. What was that?

Goldie's ears pricked. "Girls," she whispered. "I think something's outside!"

Jess leaped up and ran outside, followed by Lily and Goldie. She spotted a shadowy shape among the trees.

"Over there!" Jess pointed, but the shadow had gone.

They went back inside, and Goldie made mugs of hot honey-milk.

Bella snuffled softly. She hadn't heard a thing.

"That was strange," Lily murmured as they settled back among the blankets. She stroked the sleeping kitten anxiously. "I hope Grizelda and her Boggits aren't back in the forest." Her mind whirring, Lily drifted off into an uneasy sleep.

## CHAPTER THREE

# Footprints

The next morning, Lily woke first. When she saw the cave roof, she wondered where she was. Then she remembered.

*Goldie's grotto*, she thought with a smile. *I wonder if Bella's awake yet.*

She rolled over to see. But Bella wasn't there.

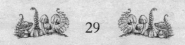

Lily shook Jess and Goldie awake.
"I can't find Bella," she told them.

"She's probably burrowed under the
covers," said Goldie.

They searched among the quilts and
blankets and called Bella's name. But
there was no sign of the little kitten.

Jess's hands flew to her mouth. "She's
gone!" she cried.

Lily pointed to an empty hook.
"Her backpack's gone, too," she
exclaimed.

Lily went pale. "Remember the noises
we heard last night? Maybe Bella woke

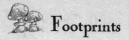 

up and heard them, too, and went to
find out what was making them!"

Goldie's whiskers twitched with
worry. "Let's hurry back to Toadstool
Glade," she said. "If Bella's gone
off exploring, someone might have
seen her."

She grabbed her scarf. Outside, they
saw that it had rained heavily in the
night. Raindrops sparkled on the leaves
of the Blossom Briar.

"I hope poor Bella didn't get soaked,"
said Lily as they hurried after Goldie.

At Toadstool Glade, Goldie jumped on

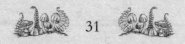

a log and called to all the animals. "Has anyone seen Bella Tabbypaw?"

"Not since yesterday," said Mrs. Twinkletail the mouse.

Mrs. Longwhiskers nodded. "The last time we saw her was when she left for the sleepover."

Goldie frowned thoughtfully. "Has anyone heard anything strange in the forest? Or seen anything odd? It might help us find out where Bella is."

A duckling wearing red boots waddled forward. It was Ellie Featherbill! The girls had stopped Grizelda and her Boggits

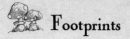 

from ruining
Willowtree
River, where
the Featherbills
lived. Ellie's seven
brothers and
sisters, also wearing
brightly colored
boots, waddled
after her.

"We've just been playing in puddles,"
Ellie said shyly. "My brother Stanley saw
footprints in the mud. Big ones! Come
and see!"

When
Goldie and the
girls reached the spot
in the forest where the ducklings
were playing, they found four sets of large
footprints and one set of tiny paw prints.

They stared at one another in horror.

"There's only one kind of creature that could have made those big prints," said Goldie grimly. "Boggits!"

"Four Boggits and Bella," said Lily in dismay. "Do you think they've kidnapped her, like they did to Lucy Longwhiskers?"

"I'm afraid it looks like it," said Goldie.

"Come on," said Jess.

"We've got to get Bella back!"

They thanked the Featherbill ducklings

for their help and set off to follow the

prints through the forest. They were soon

deep among the trees.

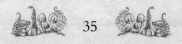

"Let's hurry," said Goldie, glancing up at the sky. "It looks like it's going to rain again."

Sure enough, moments later, fat raindrops began to fall.

"We'll be soaking wet soon," said Lily, shaking water from her bangs.

Jess stopped and pointed. "Oh, no—the rain's washing the footprints away!"

To their dismay, the prints were disappearing before their eyes. They hurried on, now unsure if they were going the right way.

"Where can Bella be?" Lily wondered

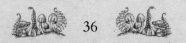 36

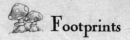

aloud. "She must be so scared." She stopped to peer through the falling rain. "There aren't so many trees here, are there? It's almost as if we're coming to—"

"The edge of Friendship Forest!" said Goldie in alarm. "I've never been this far before. Oh, girls, I'm so sorry. I don't know where Bella is, and I don't know where we are, either! This place smells horrible."

Jess comforted the tearful cat while Lily took a look around. She pushed through straggly bushes and gasped as her foot sank into something squishy.

Before her was a vast, oozing pool of runny, yellow-brown mud. Bubbles rose to the surface and popped, sending up stinking greenish clouds of gas. It smelled like old drains.

"Help!" she cried. "My foot's stuck in a swamp!"

## CHAPTER FOUR

# Boulder Barrier

"Lily! Hold on!" Jess cried.

Goldie grasped Jess around the waist
to stop her from slipping into the swamp,
too, and Jess reached out a hand to Lily.
Lily clutched it. Together, Jess and Goldie
pulled her free of the swamp.

Lily pushed back her dripping hair

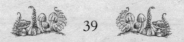

and wiped mud off her pants with wet leaves. "Thank you!" she said. "But now we're filthy, as well as soaked!"

Jess used a stick to scrape her sneaker clean, and Goldie shook glistening water droplets from her fur.

"Now what?" Lily said. "We can't go any farther, because of the swamp."

"The Boggits and Bella can't have come this way, either. Let's go back to where we last saw footprints," Jess suggested.

It had stopped raining, but they had to splash through lots of puddles on their way back to where the prints had been.

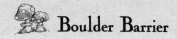 

"I definitely saw a print here," said
Jess, stopping.

The path split into three directions. One
led to the swamp and another went back
to the Toadstool Glade.

Goldie pointed down the third path.
"They must have gone down there.
Come on!"

The three friends ran along the path.
It took them past thick, stumpy trees,
across a leafy glade, and alongside a
bubbling stream. They skittered down
a slope between prickly berry bushes, but
found their way blocked by a huge heap

of large

gray boulders.

"It's a dead

end," groaned Lily.

"They're not here."

"All this way for

nothing," Jess said sadly.

She went to sit on

the nearest boulder.

"Stop!" Lily cried, pulling her back.

"What's wrong?" asked Goldie.

"Look carefully at that boulder,"
said Lily.

Goldie and Jess peered at it.

"It's shimmering," said Goldie.
"The boulder's magic!"

Lily reached out
to feel it, but her

hand passed right through! "It's all right," she said. "It doesn't hurt."

Goldie looked closer and gasped. "Girls, remember the legend I was telling you last night?" she said excitedly. "I think we've found the entrance to the Friendship Forest tunnels!"

Lily stared. "So it's true!"

"Why would the Boggits go in there?" Jess asked.

Lily frowned thoughtfully. "Remember the strange noises we heard right before the Longwhiskers' pans were knocked over? And then outside Goldie's grotto?

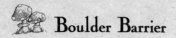 

Well, what if it was the Boggits snooping around, looking for mischief?" she said. "They would have heard Goldie talking about the jewels in the tunnels."

Jess nodded. "I think you're right—they might have decided to find the jewels! But why would they have taken Bella?"

"I don't know," said Goldie, "but we've got to go into the tunnel if we're going to get her back!"

They passed through the boulder with a shivery feeling and into the dark tunnel.

"I'll go first,"
said Goldie. "My
cat eyes give me
excellent night vision,
remember?"

She held one end of her scarf, told Lily
to hold the middle, and gave the other
end to Jess. "Now we won't get separated
in the dark," she explained.

They crept along the tunnel. Jess
and Lily felt unsteady on the rough,
uneven ground. It was strange not

being able to see their
feet very well.

A loud noise rang out
from up ahead, echoing
through the tunnels.

The three friends clung together.

"Boggits?" Lily whispered.

The sound came again, closer this time.

Goldie's ears twitched. "It's someone
laughing!" she said.

There was the pounding of running
feet, coming closer.

Goldie and the girls pressed themselves against the cold tunnel wall.

Lily clutched Jess's hand. "What is it?" she whispered.

"I don't know," Jess replied in a shaky voice.

The laughter grew louder, and shadowy shapes seemed to be moving toward them.

"Hello!" said two high little voices.

Lily and Jess sighed in relief as they peered through the gloom.

The loud, echoing noise had been made by a pair of sassy-looking fox cubs!

## CHAPTER FIVE

# Glow in the Dark

"Girls," exclaimed Goldie, "meet Ruby
and Rusty Fuzzybrush! But what are you
two doing here?"

"We use the tunnels as our secret
hiding place," said Ruby. "Mom and
Dad don't know about them, so please

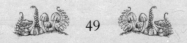

don't tell." She put down two unlit
lanterns she'd been holding.

"How did you get in?" asked Jess.
*Maybe the fox cubs found the magical entrance,
too,* she thought to herself.

"We know lots of ways," said Rusty,
"but they're all hidden. That's why
nobody else comes here."

"Somebody else has found a way in,
I'm afraid," said Goldie. She explained
about Bella and the Boggits. "If you
know the tunnels well," she added, "will
you help us find Bella?"

The fox cubs agreed immediately.

"What an adventure!" said Rusty
excitedly, picking up the lanterns. "These
might be useful. Mr. Cleverfeather
invented them."

Jess and Lily took one each and looked
for a way to turn them on.

"Where's the switch?" Jess asked.

The fox cubs laughed so hard they fell
over. "There's no switch for glowworms!"
giggled Ruby. "Watch!"

She put her mouth close to Jess's lantern
and whispered, "Wakey, wakey, little glowworms. Rise and shine! It's glowtime!"

Instantly, there was a soft glimmer

that grew brighter and brighter until the tunnel was filled with yellow light.

"Wow!" said Lily. She whispered to the glowworms in her lantern. "Wakey, wakey, rise and shine! It's glowtime!" She laughed in delight as her lantern lit up, too. The tunnel wasn't so scary now that she could see clearly.

They were about to set off again when a great gruff shout echoed down the tunnel.

"Boggits!" said Goldie, clutching at Jess and Lily. A moment later, there was a crashing sound and the whole tunnel seemed to shudder.

"It's an earthquake!" Lily whispered fearfully.

There was another crash. She covered her ears to shut out the noise.

The lanterns went dark.

"Oh, no!" Jess said. "The noise must have frightened the glowworms. It's too dark to go any farther without them."

"Glowworms," Lily whispered, "don't be frightened. It's just a noise and we won't let it hurt you. Please wakey, wakey."

There was the smallest beam of light.

"Please?" begged Lily. "Rise and shine?"

Rusty crept over. "Hey, wormies!" he whispered. "We're desperate."

There was a tiny glimmer, then another, then another. Soon the lantern was filled with glowing lights, and the girls could see again.

"What are the Boggits up to?" said Goldie. "I'm so worried about Bella! Rusty and Ruby, I know it's scary, but please take us through the tunnels so we can look for her."

Rusty and Ruby darted away.

As the others followed, Jess noticed that the light from the glowworms was

casting huge shadows
on the tunnel walls. *What are
they?* she wondered with a flutter of
fear. Then she realized! "The fox cubs'
shadows make them seem like giants!"
she laughed.

Ruby and Rusty heard.
They waved their
paws and lashed
their tails, making
their shadows
look like angry
monsters!

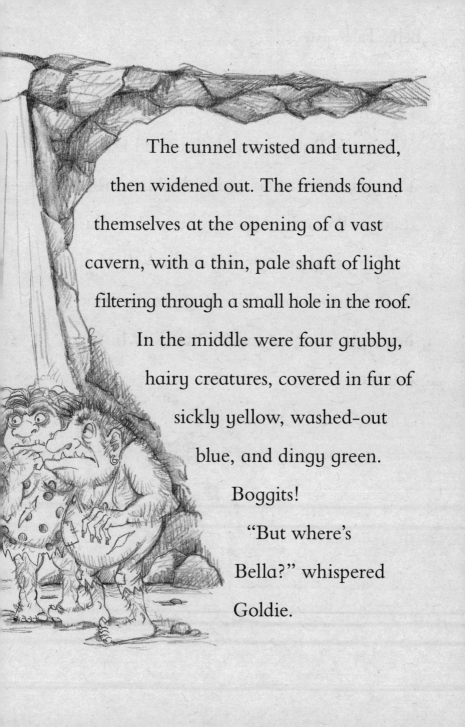

The tunnel twisted and turned,
then widened out. The friends found
themselves at the opening of a vast
cavern, with a thin, pale shaft of light
filtering through a small hole in the roof.
In the middle were four grubby,
hairy creatures, covered in fur of
sickly yellow, washed-out
blue, and dingy green.
Boggits!
"But where's
Bella?" whispered
Goldie.

Lily and Jess peered around the cavern. When the Boggits had kidnapped Lucy Longwhiskers, they had locked her inside a cage. What had they done with Bella?

Then, to their surprise, Bella walked out from behind one of the Boggits, wearing her night goggles and backpack, whistling happily!

# CHAPTER SIX

# A Terrible Plan

"At least Bella's okay," whispered Jess.
"But why is she with the Boggits? And
what are they doing down here?"

Lily asked the glowworms to switch off
and the glow faded. They all hid beneath
an overhanging rock so they could spy
on the Boggits without being seen. They

could make out lots of tall, thick stone
pillars through the gloom that looked as if
they were holding up the cavern roof.

"Those pillars are blocking the view,"
whispered Lily. She jumped as a Boggit
laughed.

"Haargh! Haargh!"

Rusty sniffed. "Pooh, those Boggits stink!"

"Like rotting cauliflowers," Jess agreed
in disgust. "Are they searching for jewels?
Can you see what they're up to, Goldie?"

"Yes," said the cat. "Whiffy's scratching
herself, Reek is picking his nose, and Sniff
and Pongo are carrying huge stones."

Pongo's voice echoed around the cavern. "Oy, kittycat," he grunted to Bella. "Put goggles on and tell Boggits where cracks are in pillars."

Bella stopped whistling. "All right," she said. After a moment, she continued. "This one's cracked."

Pongo bashed the pillar hard with his stone.

"Hegga, hegga!" chuckled Sniff. "Kittycat can see cracks with goggles. Clever Sniff to think of bringing kittycat to tunnels."

"Are we going to get some jewels

now?" Bella was pointing upward. "You

promised you'd help me find some jewels

if I helped you with my night goggles."

Jess glanced at the cave ceiling, where

Bella was pointing. She gasped.

"Look, Lily! Goldie, see

there? On the cavern roof?"

"It's glittering!"

whispered Lily.

"Jewels!" breathed

Goldie. "The roof is

studded with them,

just like the

legend said!"

"Poor Bella," whispered Lily. "She must have left Goldie's grotto to go exploring and bumped into the Boggits. They've tricked her into helping them!"

"But why are the Boggits smashing the pillars?" Jess wondered.

Whiffy gave another pillar a bash. "Boggits are right under Toadstool Glade. When pillars fall, Toadstool Glade will crash down. Bang! Smash! All animals' nasty cottages fall to bits! Grizelda be pleased!"

Jess, Lily, and Goldie clutched one another in horror!

"This is Grizelda's most terrible plan yet!" gasped Lily. "All the animals' homes will be destroyed. They'll have to leave the forest and Grizelda will have it for herself!"

Goldie quickly explained what was happening to Ruby and Rusty. "To save Friendship Forest, we've got to stop the Boggits from smashing those pillars," she said urgently.

Jess glanced at her lantern. "Lily," she said, "remember how the glowworms' light cast big shadows on the wall?"

Lily nodded.

"It's given me an idea for scaring away the Boggits," said Jess. "A shadow monster!"

"Brilliant!" said Lily. "But we can't scare Bella." She thought for a moment. "I know! Quiet, everyone!"

She picked up a stone and threw it as far as possible across the cavern. As she heard it land, the Boggits turned toward it. They'd heard it, too.

"What be that?" asked Whiffy.

"Boggits look," said Pongo. "Come on."

All four lumbered toward where the stone had landed.

In a flash, Lily darted out and scooped Bella up. The little kitten gave a happy squeak and started purring.

"Hi, Lily—" Bella started to say, but
Lily hushed her.

She darted back behind the rock,
where Jess and Goldie hugged Bella with
relief.

"Thank goodness you're safe!" said
Goldie. She explained that the Boggits

had tricked Bella into helping them with their plan.

Bella was horrified. "Knock the cottages down? Destroy Toadstool Glade?" she whispered. "I thought they were being nice. They can't ruin the village!"

"You're right," said Jess. "And we need a brave little explorer to help stop them."

## CHAPTER SEVEN

# Monster!

Jess whispered in Bella's ear.

The kitten's eyes grew wide.

"Go on," said Jess when she'd finished.
"Goggles on, you brave explorer."

Bella scampered to the middle of
the cavern just as the Boggits returned,
grumbling about mystery noises.

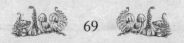

"Boggits!" cried Bella. "I've remembered something scary."

Reek snorted. "Boggits isn't scared."

The others laughed. "Haargh! Haargh!"

"Shh!" said Bella. "You'll wake it."

"Wake what?" growled Reek.

"The monster!" said Bella. "The Boggit-eating monster!"

"No such thing." Pongo scoffed.

But Sniff grunted nervously. "What if there really is monster?"

Whiffy looked down. "Whiffy's knees is knocking."

"No monster." Pongo growled.

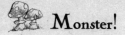 

"Kittycat, find cracked pillars. Boggits, get bashing!"

Beneath the overhanging rock, Jess explained her plan to the others.

"Bella's given them the idea of a monster," she whispered. "Now it's up to us to make one!"

They gathered in a line, arms around one another's waists. Lily and Jess were at the top, so the shadow monster would have two heads and four front legs. The fox cubs were next, so it seemed to have eight more little legs. Goldie was at the back, bent over like a great hump.

When Bella saw Lily give the
thumbs-up, she sneaked back over.

Lily whispered, "Wakey, wakey,
little glowworms. Rise and shine! It's
glowtime!" and handed the lanterns to
the plucky kitten.

Bella crept back to the Boggits.

The lantern's light grew from a

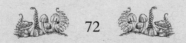

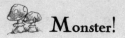 

glimmer to a golden glow. Bella shone it on the friends, casting a huge monster-shadow on the wall.

Lily and Jess roared and wobbled their heads, making the shadow heads rear back and forth. The fox cubs stamped and howled.

"Aaaargh!" screeched Reek.

"Monster attack!" shrieked Pongo. "Run!"

The shadow monster roared and lashed its tail.

"Don't eat me!" begged Sniff. "Eat Whiffy!"

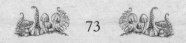

"No! I

be thin and bony,"

bellowed Whiffy. "Eat Sniff!

Sniff be tasty!"

They fought, pushed, and scrambled to

escape the monster. At last, they found a

tunnel and stampeded down it, shrieking.

The group of friends, with Bella in

tow, followed the Boggits down one

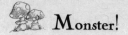 

tunnel, then another, roaring and
howling.

Goldie sniffed. "There's a horrible smell
coming from up ahead," she called over
the roars.

"That's the swamp," cried Rusty. "It's all
mud and stink."

"If we can chase them into
it," Lily said, "maybe
they'll be so happy
to find mud that
they won't come
back to smash
the pillars!"

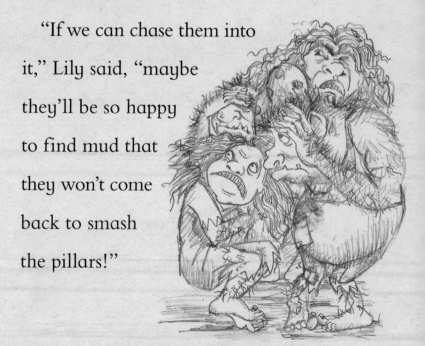

"Great idea," said Jess.

Roaring and howling some more, the
shadow monster lurched on down
the tunnel behind the Boggits. They
thundered along, shrieking in fright, and
ran out into the gray light.

Lily, Jess, Goldie, and the others waited
in the tunnel until the Boggits' yells died

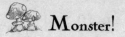 

down. Then they crept outside. The
Boggits were tramping into the swamp.

Pongo spotted them and roared in
fury. "Boggits been tricked!" he bellowed.
"Get them!"

But the other Boggits ignored him.

Whiffy grabbed handfuls of the gloop

oozing around her. "Lovely!" she said, rubbing it into her fur.

Sniff and Reek sloshed mud over each other.

"Better than Boggits' muddy pool," said Reek happily. He flung himself on his back and sank into the mud, shouting, "LOVELY swamp!" He stood up, gloop oozing down his nose.

Even Pongo agreed. "Swamp is enormous," he said and dove in head first. "Wheeee!"

"I think we're safe," Jess whispered. "Goldie, the Boggits love the swamp so much, perhaps we can talk them into staying here?"

Lily hugged her. "That's a terrific idea!" she said. "Grizelda was going to give them a new home if they ruined Friendship Forest, so they'd obviously be happy to move."

"It's a wonderful idea," Goldie agreed. "If they're happy here, they'd have no reason to do what Grizelda wants. But it will take some work to turn the swamp into the perfect Boggit home. We're going to need help."

"Send a flyer," suggested Jess. "Lots of flyers!"

Goldie put her
paws together like
wings and fluttered them.
The fox cubs and Bella did the same,
then Jess and Lily fluttered their hands.

A moment later, a large yellow
butterfly perched on Goldie's shoulder.

"Hello, Flitta," said the cat.

A purple butterfly settled

on Goldie's other shoulder.

"Hi, Hermia," said

Jess, remembering her

from their adventure

rescuing Molly Twinkletail.

Soon they were surrounded by a cloud of butterflies. Their rainbow colors swirled as they danced around one another, chattering in tiny, tinkly voices. Jess and Lily caught some of what they were saying.

"That smell! Oh, dear!"

"I know! Enough to make your wings droop."

"You can see why," trilled another. "*B-O-G-G-I-T-S.*"

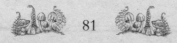

Goldie giggled. "Butterflies," she said, "please ask all the animals to bring supplies—anything suitable for a Boggit home."

As the butterflies flew away, the girls heard Hermia tell Flitta, "The animals won't have to think very hard. They can just bring their garbage cans!" and they both laughed.

## CHAPTER EIGHT

# Home, Stinky Home

Jess and Lily helped Mr. Cleverfeather put the roof on a hut for the Boggits. He'd brought a new invention, the Lifter-upper. As Jess sat on a seat and pedaled madly, the Lifter-upper raised the roof. Lily pushed a button, and the roof moved directly above the hut.

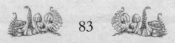

Mr. Cleverfeather pressed a button. Down it dropped. *Bang!*

The Featherbills laid down a carpet of slimy pondweed from near their river barge.

"Urgh, it's yucky," said Ellie Featherbill.

"Boggits love yuck," Lily giggled. "And muck."

Other animals heaped garbage around the hut. Pongo looked at it fondly, as Reek and Sniff splashed in the mud. Bella and the fox cubs rolled around beside them.

"The smell doesn't bother you after a while," yelled Rusty, laughing.

Just then Mr. Cleverfeather called, "The rut's heady—er, I mean the hut's ready!"

"Not ready." Whiffy grunted. "Hut needs mud." She scooped up fistfuls of swamp goo and threw it over the roof.

The other Boggits joined in happily.

Reek grunted. "Girls and cat find swamp. Girls good!"

Sniff grinned. "Cat good!"

"Mud good!" cried Whiffy.

Pongo turned to Bella. "Kittycat want to help?"

Everybody wanted to help!

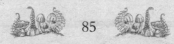

Suddenly, Lily's eye was caught by an orb of light floating across the swamp.

"Grizelda!" she cried. "Grizelda's here!"

The animals shrieked and ran to huddle behind Goldie and the girls.

The orb hovered, then, with a flash and a *cra-ack*, it burst in a shower of yellow sparks. In its place stood the witch, wearing her shiny purple tunic and pants, and her boots with their sharply pointed toes. Her green hair swirled around her head like snakes.

"Boggits!" she screeched. "Get back to work. Go and smash those pillars!"

There was a moment's silence. The
Boggits muttered together.

"Oh, no," Lily whispered. "They're
going to obey her."

"We can't let them," said Jess.
"Boggits!" she yelled. "You have a
new home. You don't need to do what
she says!"

Pongo looked at Jess. He looked at
the dirty new hut. Then he turned to
Grizelda. "No!" he shouted. "Boggits not
helping *anymore*!"

Reek lumbered forward. "Grizelda
smash pillars herself." He growled.

"What!" shrieked Grizelda. "Me? Work? Are you crazy? You do it!"

Lily and Jess held their breath. Would the Boggits give in?

"No!" Whiffy snapped, peering from behind Sniff.

Grizelda screamed, "If you want a new home, get rid of the animals first—"

"No!" said Pongo. "Boggits is happy in swamp. Go away!"

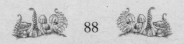

Grizelda's hair whipped the air. Her face was dark with rage. "I won't give up," she snarled. "Friendship Forest will be mine!"

She snapped her fingers and vanished in a shower of hissing red sparks.

The animals cheered. "Hooray for the Boggits!"

"Thank goodness she's gone," said Lily, then she gasped. "But what about the damage the Boggits did to the cavern? What if they've already done enough to harm the forest?"

"Oh, we stopped them before any serious damage was done," said Goldie.

"I'll go and check later to make sure, but
I think Toadstool Glade will be just fine."

"Hooray! The forest is safe!" Lily cried.

But Jess noticed a flicker of worry cross
Goldie's face. "What is it?" she asked.

"I think Grizelda meant what she said,"
Goldie said nervously. "She won't give up
until she has the forest for herself."

Lily gave her a hug.
"Then we'll do our
best to stop her. We
promise!"

Jess hugged Goldie, too.
"You can count on us!"

The animals waved good-bye to the Boggits, then set off home. The Boggits sat in the swamp, patting mud into their fur. They grinned at Goldie and the girls, showing their filthy teeth.

"I can't believe we're sort-of friends with them now." Lily giggled.

"Me neither," said Jess. "They're all right when they're not obeying Grizelda, aren't they? Dirty, of course."

"And smelly," Lily said.

"And hideous and lumpy," said Goldie.

"But kind of nice, too," Jess added, and they laughed.

It was time to leave the swamp. Jess picked up a purring Bella, and Lily held the fox cubs' paws. Overhead, the butterflies fluttered like a rainbow cloud.

Back in Toadstool Glade, the animals threw a party to celebrate. There was lots of yummy food from the Toadstool Café and everyone danced to music coming from a strange box that Mr. Cleverfeather called his Melody-o-Matic. Lily, Jess, and Goldie whirled around. Bella swished her tail in time to the music and the Longwhiskers family danced the bunny hop, which included lots of hopping.

Eventually, it was time for Lily and Jess to go home.

"My mom and dad won't believe how much exploring I did," said Bella as they gave her a farewell cuddle. "Thank you for rescuing me."

"You're very welcome," said Lily. They waved good-bye to their other friends and followed Goldie to the Friendship Tree at the center of the forest.

When they reached it, Goldie said, "I'm so proud of you for helping to stop Grizelda. When I first saw you at the wildlife hospital, I knew I could

count on such brave, kind girls." She
hugged them.

"We've had such wonderful adventures,"
said Jess.

"I'll come back for you soon," Goldie
promised. She touched a paw to the
tree and a door appeared in the trunk.
"Good-bye for now, girls!"

"Good-bye!" said Lily and Jess. Holding
hands, they stepped through the door and
into the golden light. When it faded, they
were back in Brightley Meadow.

"What an amazing adventure," sighed
Jess as they went over the stepping-stones

and back to Helping Paw. "I'm so glad the forest is safe."

"Me, too," agreed Lily.

Although the girls had been gone all night and much of that day, no time had passed in their world. At the wildlife hospital, the kittens were just waking up.

"They're so cute," said Lily. "The smallest one looks a bit like Bella, doesn't she?"

"She does," said Jess. "Oh, Lily, she's so sweet. I wish—"

She stopped as the door opened, and Mr. Forester came in, clutching his mug of tea.

"Jess, I've been thinking," he said. "We'll

need to find homes for all these kittens. Maybe one of them could live with us."

She threw her arms around him. "Oh, thanks, Dad!" she cried. "I'd really love the tiny one!"

Lily lifted the kitten into Jess's hands. As the little creature purred, the girls shared a secret smile. What a magical day!

## The End

# Lily and Jess's Animal Care Tips

Lily and Jess love helping lots of different animals—both in Friendship Forest and in the real world.

Here are their top tips for looking after . . .

## CATS

like Bella Tabbypaw.

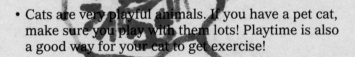

- Cats are very playful animals. If you have a pet cat, make sure you play with them lots! Playtime is also a good way for your cat to get exercise!

- All cats like milk, but it is not good for them to have too much of it.

- Cats like to roam over a wide area. If you find a cat that you think might be a stray, the best thing to do is to ask around the neighborhood to see if anyone knows who the cat belongs to.

# Puzzle Fun!

One of our Magic Animal Friends
is hiding in this picture.

Can you connect the dots to discover who it is?

When best friends Lily and Jess visit Friendship Forest, they'll need to rescue baby bunny Lucy Longwhiskers from the witch Grizelda!
Join them on their first adventure!

# Lucy Longwhiskers
# Gets Lost

Grizelda is still trying to take over Friendship Forest and now her horrible Boggits have played a mean trick on little Molly Twinkletail!

Join Lily, Jess, and Molly in the next adventure,

# Molly Twinkletail Runs Away

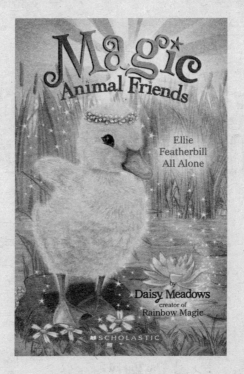

Grizelda is still causing trouble in Friendship Forest and now her Boggits are planning to poison the river! Can Lily and Jess stop them?

Find out in their next adventure,

# Ellie Featherbill All Alone

# RAINBOW magic ™

# Which Magical Fairies Have You Met?

- ❑ The Rainbow Fairies
- ❑ The Weather Fairies
- ❑ The Jewel Fairies
- ❑ The Pet Fairies
- ❑ The Dance Fairies
- ❑ The Music Fairies
- ❑ The Sports Fairies
- ❑ The Party Fairies
- ❑ The Ocean Fairies
- ❑ The Night Fairies
- ❑ The Magical Animal Fairies
- ❑ The Princess Fairies
- ❑ The Superstar Fairies
- ❑ The Fashion Fairies
- ❑ The Sugar & Spice Fairies
- ❑ The Earth Fairies

## ▬ SCHOLASTIC

Find all of your favorite fairy friends at
**scholastic.com/rainbowmagic**

RMFAIRY10

# RAINBOW magic™

## SPECIAL EDITION

# Which Magical Fairies Have You Met?

**3 stories in each one!**

- ☐ Joy the Summer Vacation Fairy
- ☐ Holly the Christmas Fairy
- ☐ Kylie the Carnival Fairy
- ☐ Stella the Star Fairy
- ☐ Shannon the Ocean Fairy
- ☐ Trixie the Halloween Fairy
- ☐ Gabriella the Snow Kingdom Fairy
- ☐ Juliet the Valentine Fairy
- ☐ Mia the Bridesmaid Fairy
- ☐ Flora the Dress-Up Fairy
- ☐ Paige the Christmas Play Fairy
- ☐ Emma the Easter Fairy
- ☐ Cara the Camp Fairy
- ☐ Destiny the Rock Star Fairy
- ☐ Belle the Birthday Fairy
- ☐ Olympia the Games Fairy
- ☐ Selena the Sleepover Fairy
- ☐ Cheryl the Christmas Tree Fairy
- ☐ Florence the Friendship Fairy
- ☐ Lindsay the Luck Fairy
- ☐ Brianna the Tooth Fairy
- ☐ Autumn the Falling Leaves Fairy
- ☐ Keira the Movie Star Fairy
- ☐ Addison the April Fool's Day Fairy
- ☐ Bailey the Babysitter Fairy

## ■SCHOLASTIC

Find all of your favorite fairy friends at
**scholastic.com/rainbowmagic**

HIT entertainment

RMSPECIAL13

# The Rescue Princesses

These are no ordinary princesses—
they're Rescue Princesses!